STAR WARS®

CLONE WARS

ADVENTURES

VOLUME 2

designer
Joshua Elliott

assistant editor
Dave Marshall

editors
Jeremy Barlow
Randy Stradley

publisher
Mike Richardson

special thanks to Sue Rostoni and Amy Gary
at Lucas Licensing

◆ The events in this story take place approximately
five months after the Battle of Geonosis

www.titanbooks.com
www.starwars.com

STAR WARS: CLONE WARS ADVENTURES volume 2, November 2004.
Published by Titan Books, a division of Titan Publishing Group Ltd. 144 Southwark Street,
London SE1 0UP. Star Wars ©2004 Lucasfilm Ltd. & ™. All rights reserved. Used under
authorisation. Used under authorisation. Text and illustrations for Star Wars are © 2004 Lucasfilm Ltd.
No portion of this publication may be reproduced or transmitted, in any form or by any means,
without the express written permission of the copyright holder, Inc. Names, characters, places
and incidents featured in this publication either are the product of the author's imagination or
are used fictitiously. Any resemblance to actual persons (living or dead), events, institutions, or
locales, without satiric intent, is coincidental. Printed in China

STAR WARS®

CLONE WARS

ADVENTURES

VOLUME 2

"SKYWALKERS"

script **Haden Blackman**

Additional dialogue by George Lucas

From *Star Wars*: Episode IV *A New Hope*

art **The Fillbach Brothers**

colors **Wil Glass**

"HIDE IN PLAIN SIGHT"

script **Welles Hartley**

art **The Fillbach Brothers**

colors **SnoCone Studios**

"RUN MACE RUN"

script and art **The Fillbach Brothers**

colors **Wil Glass**

lettering
Michael David Thomas

cover
The Fillbach Brothers and Dan Jackson

TATOOINE, 19 YEARS AFTER THE BATTLE OF CORUSCANT.

YOU FOUGHT IN THE CLONE WARS?

YES. I WAS ONCE A JEDI KNIGHT, THE SAME AS YOUR FATHER.

I WISH I'D KNOWN HIM...

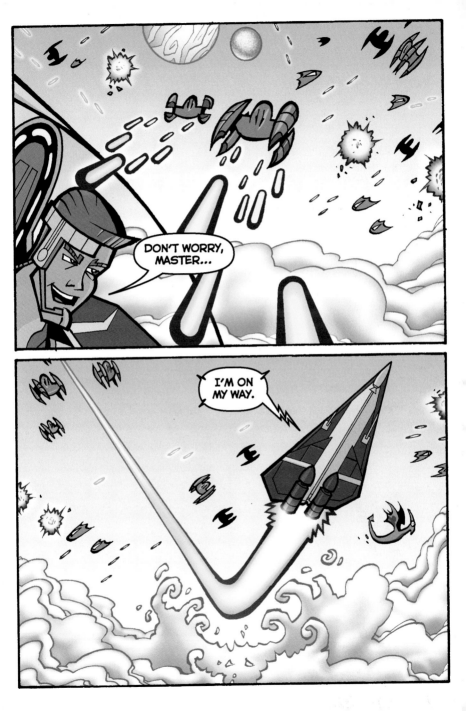

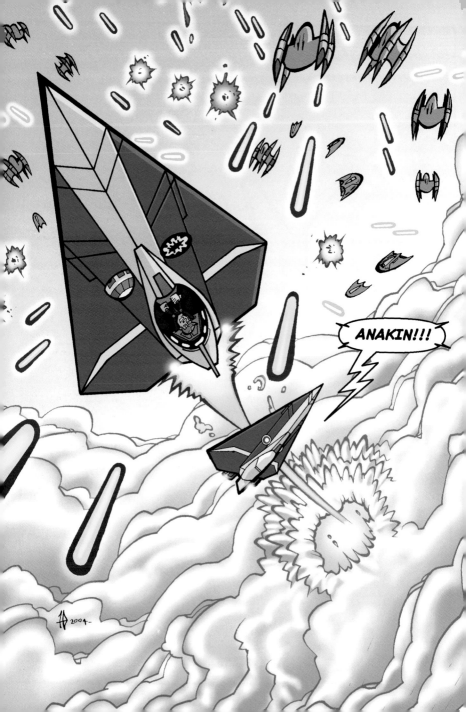

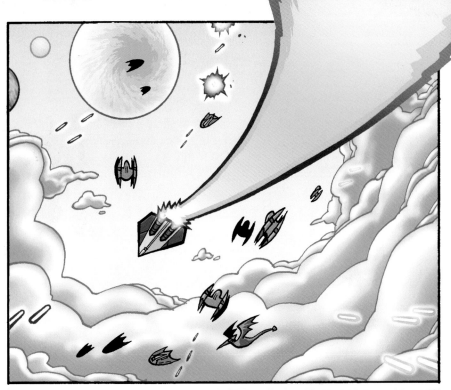

I'M GLAD YOU'RE SO CONFIDENT...

ESPECIALLY SINCE THIS PLANET'S ATMOSPHERE IS WREAKING HAVOC WITH MY SENSORS.

I'M FLYING BLI --

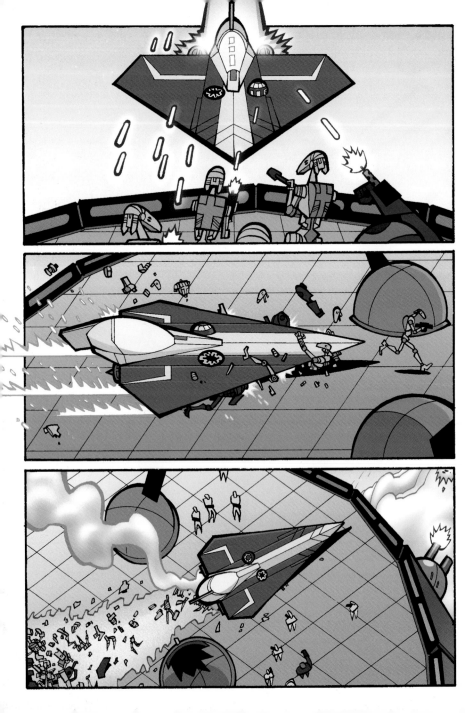

ANAKIN, WHAT'S YOUR STATUS?

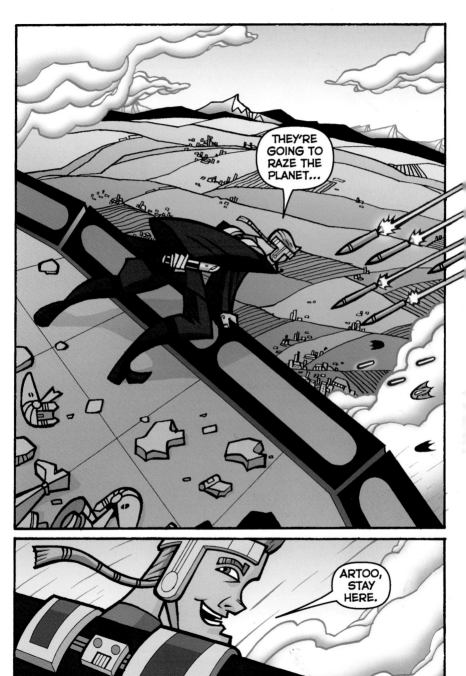

NEAR THE REMAINS OF ALDERAAN...

THE HEIGHT OF THE GALACTIC CIVIL WAR.

THREADNEEDLE CANYON, NADIEM. FIVE MONTHS AFTER THE BATTLE OF GEONOSIS.

LUMINARA UNDULI AND BARRISS OFFEE IN

HIDE IN

PLAIN

SIGHT

A *CLONE WARS* ADVENTURE

FALL BACK TO THE NEXT MARKER.

ADVANCE SQUAD TO *GENERAL UNDULI...*

...THE DROID ARMY HAS QUICKENED ITS PACE. E.T.A. AT YOUR LOCATION IN LESS THAN ONE HOUR.

MESSAGE RECEIVED, COMMANDER. PROCEED AS ORDERED.

WORRIED ABOUT THE BATTLE, MASTER?

NO, *BARRISS.* I HAVE EVERY CONFIDENCE IN OUR ARMY, BUT I WANTED TO GET THE CIVILIANS CLEAR BEFORE THE FIGHTING BEGAN.

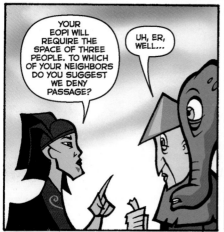

THE JEDI IS RIGHT. GETTING OUR FAMILIES TO SAFETY IS MORE IMPORTANT THAT ANYTHING WE MIGHT OWN.

THANK YOU.

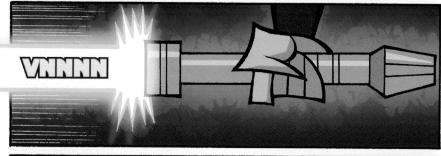

VNNNN

NO!

SW-I-I-K!

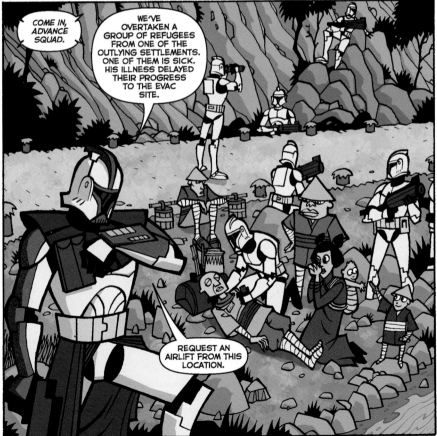

MASTER, LET ME GO. IF WE MOVE QUICKLY, WE CAN STILL GET THE VILLAGERS TO SAFETY BEFORE THE SEPARATIST ARMY ARRIVES!

"ALL RIGHT, BARRISS. GO. BUT TAKE ALONG A SQUAD OF COMMANDOS. I WANT TO BE CERTAIN THAT YOU RETURN SAFELY, PADAWAN."

THE VILLAGER'S TRANSPORT HAS ARRIVED, COMMANDER! LET'S GET THEM ON BOARD!

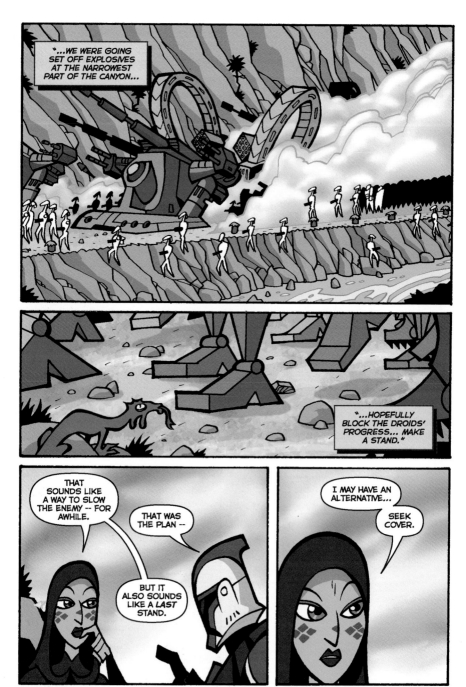

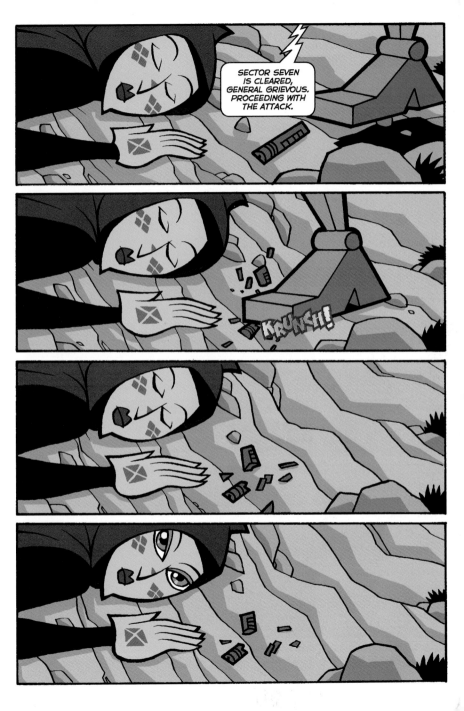

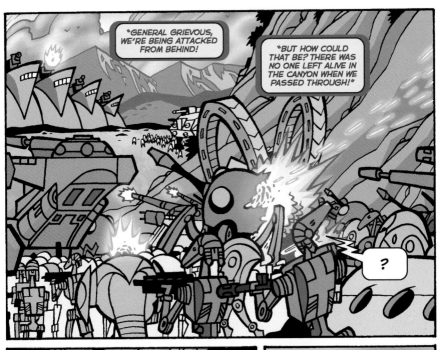

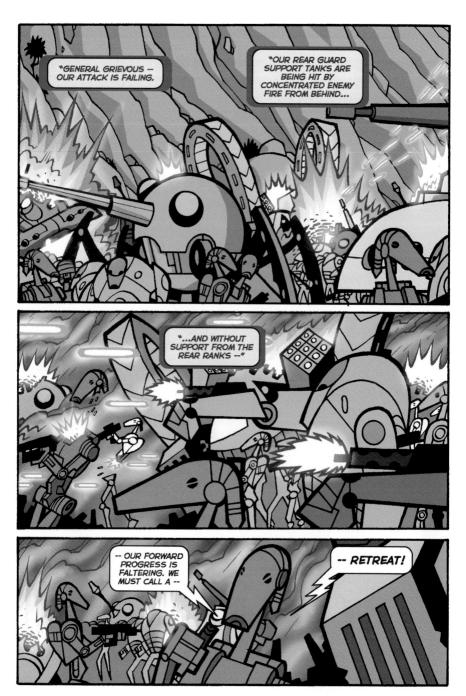

STAR WARS

CLONE WARS
ADVENTURES

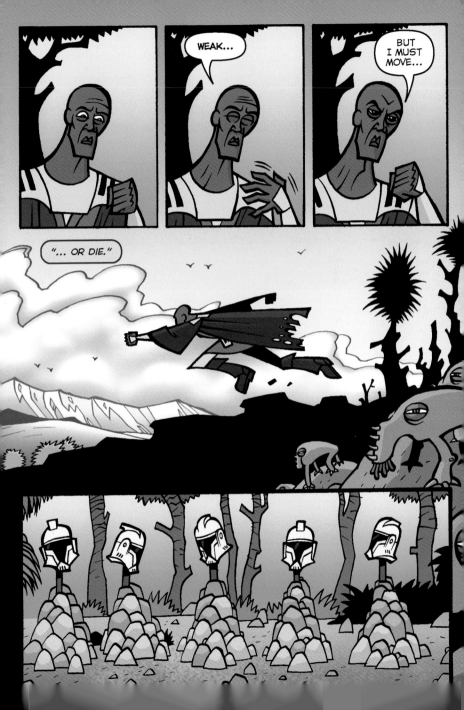

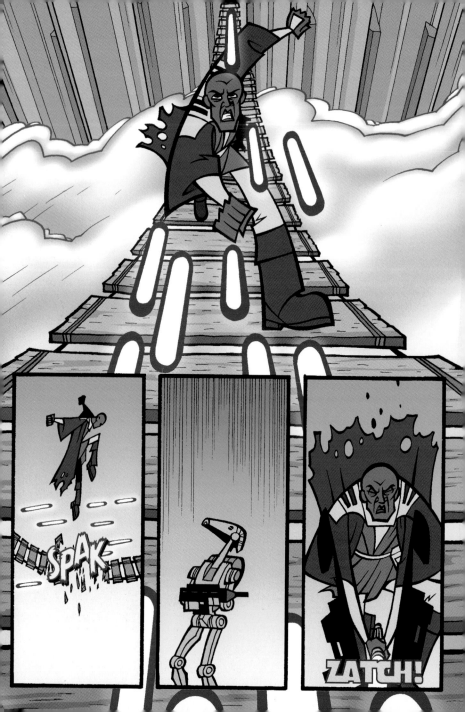

STAR WARS

 GRAPHIC NOVELS FROM TITAN BOOKS

MOVIE STAR WARS EPISODE I	MOVIE STAR WARS EPISODE II	MOVIE STAR WARS EPISODE III
PHANTOM MENACE 32 BSW4	ATTACK OF THE CLONES 22 BSW4	19 BSW 4

SITH ERA

PREQUEL I, II, III

Star Wars: Tales of the Jedi –
The Collection (feat. Knights
of the Old Republic) 4000 BSW4

Star Wars: Tales of the Jedi
– The Sith War 3998 BSW4

Star Wars: Tales of the Jedi
– Redemption 3996 BSW4

Star Wars: Jedi Vs. Sith
1000 BSW4

52 BSW4 Star Wars: Jango Fett
– Open Seasons
Star Wars: Jedi Council – Acts
of War 33 BSW4

Star Wars: Prelude to
Rebellion 33 BSW4

Star Wars: Darth Maul
33 BSW4

Star Wars:
Bounty Hunters 32 ASW4

Star Wars: Episode I
Phantom Menace 32 BSW4

Star Wars: Episode I Adventures
32 BSW4

Star Wars: Outlander 32 BSW4

Star Wars: Emissaries to
Malastare 32 BSW4

Star Wars: Darkness 31 BSW4

Star Wars: Twilight 31 BSW4

Star Wars: The Hunt for Aurra
Sing 30 BSW4

Star Wars: Episode II Attack of
the Clones 22 BSW4

Star Wars: Episode II
Villains Pack
(Jango Fett, Zam Wesell)
22 BSW4

Star Wars: The Clone Wars
– The Defense of Kamino
22 BSW4

Star Wars: The Clone Wars
Victories & Sacrifices 22 BSW4

Star Wars: Boba Fett – Enemy
of the Empire 3 BSW4

Star Wars: Underworld –
The Yavin Vassilika 1 BSW4

STAR WARS

 ## GRAPHIC NOVELS FROM TITAN BOOKS

MOVIE STAR WARS EPISODE IV A NEW HOPE 0 SW4	MOVIE STAR WARS EPISODE V THE EMPIRE STRIKES BACK 3 ASW4	MOVIE STAR WARS EPISODE VI RETURN OF THE JEDI 4 ASW4